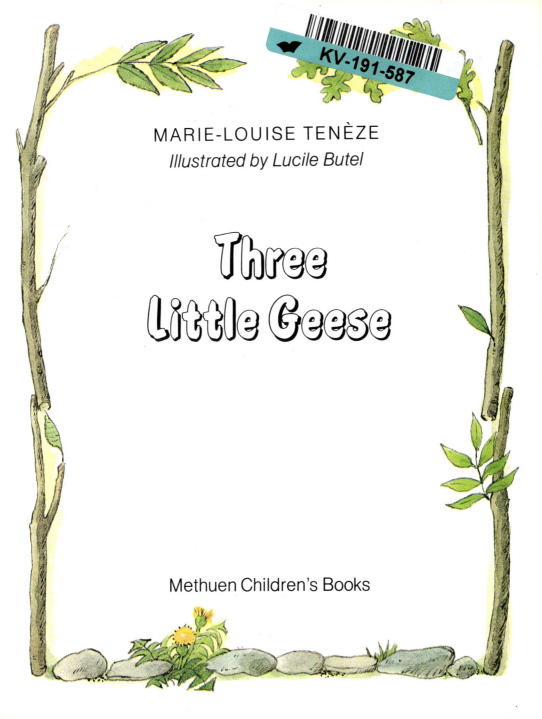

MARIE-LOUISE TENÈZE

Illustrated by Lucile Butel

Three
Little Geese

Methuen Children's Books

Once upon time there were three little
geese who were eating grass in a meadow,

when Fox came trotting past. 'What do you think you're doing here?' he asked.

'We're eating the fresh green grass.'

'Don't you know that this meadow belongs to me? I'll be back in a while, and if you're still here then, I'll eat you all up.'

The little geese put their heads together and wondered what they should do. The eldest goose said to the youngest goose, 'Won't you help me make a little house, and then I'll help you make one too.'

So the youngest goose
helped the eldest goose.

But when the house of the eldest goose
was finished, she shut herself in and
refused to help the youngest goose.

Then the youngest goose said to the smallest goose, 'Won't you help me make a little house? You saw what your sister did to me: I helped her, and now she won't help me.'
   'Oh, but *I'll* help you, if you'll help me.'

But the youngest goose did the same
as the eldest goose had done.
The smallest goose helped her and

when her house was finished the youngest
goose shut herself in. And the smallest goose
was left all alone. She began to cry.

A carpenter happened to be passing by.
'Why are you crying, little goose?' he asked.

'I helped the others to make their houses,
because Fox is coming to eat us all up,
and now they won't help me!'

The carpenter felt sorry for her and began
to make her a little house. And on the door

he fixed some nails which, instead of
pointing inwards, pointed outwards.

And when it was finished he said, 'Step inside, and let Fox come: you'll be safe.'

Only a few minutes had passed when Fox
arrived. He knocked at the house of the
smallest goose, but the little goose did not
open her door. Fox was so annoyed he
decided to break the door down …

But he stabbed himself on the nails and
ran away howling across the meadows.